Dear Parents:

Congratulations! Your child is taking the first steps on an exciting journey. The destination? Independent reading!

STEP INTO READING® will help your child get there. The program offers five steps to reading success. Each step includes fun stories and colorful art or photographs. In addition to original fiction and books with favorite characters, there are Step into Reading Non-Fiction Readers, Phonics Readers and Boxed Sets, Sticker Readers, and Comic Readers—a complete literacy program with something to interest every child.

Learning to Read, Step by Step!

Ready to Read   Preschool–Kindergarten
• **big type and easy words** • **rhyme and rhythm** • **picture clues**
For children who know the alphabet and are eager to begin reading.

Reading with Help   Preschool–Grade 1
• **basic vocabulary** • **short sentences** • **simple stories**
For children who recognize familiar words and sound out new words with help.

Reading on Your Own   Grades 1–3
• **engaging characters** • **easy-to-follow plots** • **popular topics**
For children who are ready to read on their own.

Reading Paragraphs   Grades 2–3
• **challenging vocabulary** • **short paragraphs** • **exciting stories**
For newly independent readers who read simple sentences with confidence.

Ready for Chapters   Grades 2–4
• **chapters** • **longer paragraphs** • **full-color art**
For children who want to take the plunge into chapter books but still like colorful pictures.

STEP INTO READING® is designed to give every child a successful reading experience. The grade levels are only guides; children will progress through the steps at their own speed, developing confidence in their reading. The F&P Text Level on the back cover serves as another tool to help you choose the right book for your child.

Remember, a lifetime love of reading starts with a single step!

JOHN CENA

MY MONSTER TRUCK FAMILY

Cover illustrated by Howard McWilliam
Interior illustrated by Dave Aikins

Random House 🏠 New York

I have four brothers.
They are also
monster trucks!

This is Tank.

He is big!

This is Flash.

He is fast.

VROOM!

This is Pinball.

He is smart.

13

This is Crash.

He is wild.

This is Mel.

She built us all!

We are a monster truck family!

When one of us

gets dirty,

we all help
clean him up!

When one of us

gets hurt,

OUCH-A-ROO!

22

we all help

fix him up!

we all help
cheer him up!

YAY!

we make

him soup!

27

We take care
of each other.

Plus, we get to
play together.

CRASH!

SPLASH!